Daugherty Park Merry-Go-Round

Daugherty Park Merry-Go-Round

By DC Fidler

Published by DCFidler Publishing

2022

Published by DCFidler Publishing
1117 University Avenue, #505
Morgantown, WV 26505
DCFidlerpublishing@gmail.com

Printed in the United States of America
by Kindle Direct Publishing

10, 9, 8, 7, 6, 5, 4, 3, 2, 1

This play is entirely a work of fiction.
Any resemblance to actual persons, living or dead,
is entirely coincidental.

ISBN: 979-8-9855209-5-8 (paperback)
ISBN: 979-8-9855209-6-5 (ebook)

Appreciation

Thank you Stacey Meeker for suggesting that I take a two-character scene from an exercise that I created in my textbook, and expand it into a full play. It worked!

Thank you Travis Teffner for once again dreaming characters with me.

Thank you Sandi Constantino-Thompson for your endless enthusiasm and energy in editing and suggesting.

It is wonderful to have all of you as colleagues and friends enjoying the journey.

Daugherty Park Merry-Go-Round

by DC Fidler

Setting

Daugherty, North Carolina. Daugherty is home to Daugherty Pickles, Inc., one of the largest pickle farms, canneries, and distributors in the United States. It is the summer of 2013.

The production can be done on a simple black stage with few props, having cardboard abstracts of playful images such as: a courthouse, food cart, a fireplace, an office desk, a log, bushes, etc. to place mid-stage for simple scene changes.

Characters

- **Angus Winslow Daugherty Fletcher**: Younger Fletcher brother, age 20, son of Gilbert Fletcher. Angus's mother's family was the wealthiest family in Daugherty. Angus is power of attorney for his older brother, GJ. Angus spends very little money, choosing to live a simple life. He lives with GJ in a small house and collects turtle shells. He runs a small organic gardening company. Although raised in Daugherty, he works to not have a Southern accent and to use proper grammar as he dreams of leaving Daugherty.

- **GJ Fletcher**: Older Fletcher brother, age 24. His full name is Gilbert Ralph Fletcher Jr. He was born with mathematic, social-skill, abstract thinking, and motor-skill deficits. He is skilled at memorizing details such as a list of the scientific names of spiders. He collects spiders. When he becomes excited, he flaps his hands, and when he is angry at himself, he slaps the top of his head. GJ always carries a small backpack.

- **Estelle:** late 50s or early 60s, a town council woman who was a close friend with Gil's deceased wife, Louise. She wields much political pull in Daugherty. Her wealth comes from her interstate rose supply business.

- **James:** early 20s, from Mid-West, a food vendor who has been in Daugherty for one week. He travels with his girlfriend Shannon as they work carnivals and circuses. He is a con artist.

- **Shannon:** mid 20s, from New York or New Jersey, a food vendor who sometimes dates James and performs con jobs with him. She is a sucker for anyone extending true kindness, a rarity in her conflicted life. She goes by many aliases, of which "Shannon" is one. Sometimes she imitates a Southern accent to manipulate people.

- **Gil Fletcher:** late 50s or early 60s. He is the father of GJ and Angus. After his wife Louise died, he became a recluse and began drinking and reading conspiracy theory books.

Props

- Park bench
- Vendor food cart with various supplies
- Large envelope
- Ice-cream cones
- Taco
- Money
- Cup
- Picnic blanket
- Picnic basket
- Small stick to use to draw in dirt
- Three pickle jars or bottles
- Toothpicks
- Apron
- Toe-nail polish
- Desk with two chairs
- Small stuffed whale toy
- Two beach towels
- Magazine
- Magnifying glass
- Office papers
- Pistol
- Empty whiskey bottle
- Purple mailbox
- Bush - large enough to partially hide behind
- Log to sit on
- Table with plate, utensils
- Roses
- Shovels
- Bowl of ice cream
- Mason jar and lid
- Toy blue plastic ring
- Two Lone-Ranger masks
- Pail

Premier Production

Daugherty Park Merry-Go-Round was first presented as a public reading at M.T. Pockets Theatre in Morgantown, WV on November 19, 2016.

CAST

Angus: Travis Teffner
GJ: Justin Grow
Estelle: Cynthia Ulrich
James: Adam Messenger
Shannon: Tracy Nicole Lynch
Gil: Bobby Wolf

Stage Direction Reader: Mara Monaghan
Director: DC Fidler
Producer: Vickie Trickett

DAUGHERTY PARK MERRY-GO-ROUND

ACT ONE

SCENE ONE

Setting: Outside of courthouse. A summer day. GJ and ANGUS are walking along Brine Street. ANGUS is carrying a large envelope.

ANGUS: Do you have my change?

GJ: I ain't got change, Angus.

ANGUS: I gave you a dollar bill to buy 25 cents worth of Juicy Fruit.

GJ: I ain't got change.

ANGUS: Juicy Fruit costs one quarter.

GJ: I ain't got one quarter.

ANGUS: How many quarters in a dollar? We went over this a million times.

GJ: A million quarters.

ANGUS: Four quarters. Four quarters, GJ. Each quarter is worth 25 cents. Juicy Fruit costs 25 cents. Juicy Fruit costs one quarter.

GJ: One. I should'a brung back one quarter. Cuz I used up another quarter on the claw-grab machine. But I ain't could grab that little polar bear.

ANGUS: Then you should have two quarters to give me.

GJ: I don't know where they gone.

ANGUS: *(Sighs)* When we go to Aunt Phoebe's tonight, I want you to be polite.

GJ: I am polite, Angus.

ANGUS: Last time we ate with her, you insulted her

something awful.

GJ: How'd I awful insult her?

ANGUS: She offered you her favorite-recipe red velvet cake and you insulted it.

GJ: Uh uh. I tode her, "No thank you, ma'am."

ANGUS: You told her, "No thank you, Aunt Phoebe, ma'am, I tasted your red velvet cake last time we was here."

GJ: I wuz polite.

ANGUS: That was not polite.

GJ: I minded my … what do you call 'em?

ANGUS: Ps and Qs. You minded your Ps and Qs.

GJ: Jes like you learnt me.

ANGUS: Taught! Taught you.

GJ: And I taught it from you real good.

(ANGUS sighs)

GJ: You mad at me, Angus?

ANGUS: How can I stay mad at you?

GJ: I don't want you mad at me.

ANGUS: I'm not mad at you.

GJ: Say you promise.

ANGUS: I promise.

GJ: Say all of it.

ANGUS: I promise Gilbert Ralph Fletcher Jr., I am not mad at you. Happy now?

GJ: I can't stand when you git mad at me.

ANGUS: Lord do I know.

GJ: Say where you're takin' me.

ANGUS: You know where.

GJ: Say it.

ANGUS: Daugherty Park.

GJ: Granddaddy Daugherty's name. And what'll you do to me?

ANGUS: Push you on the merry-go-round.

GJ: Say how.

ANGUS: You know how.

GJ: Say it.

ANGUS: Round and round.

GJ: Three rounds, Angus.

ANGUS: Round and round and round.

(GJ flaps his hands with excitement)

GJ: You're the best little brother, Angus.

ANGUS: That I sure am. Stop flapping.

GJ: Theraphosidae, Phoneutria, Argiope Aurantia, Latrodectus Geometrius—

ANGUS: —You can't make change for chewing gum, but you can name every species of spider.

GJ: Pisaurina Mira.

ANGUS: You're missing your spiders.

(GJ, still agitated, shakes his head up and down several times)

ANGUS: We'll go home soon and you can see them.

GJ: *(Rapidly)* Life is good life is good life is good life is good—

ANGUS: —Do you have your book in your backpack?

GJ: What?

ANGUS: *Charlotte's Web.*

GJ: Uh huh.

ANGUS: What's the spider's name?

GJ: Charlotte.

ANGUS: And the pig?

GJ: Wilbur.

ANGUS: And Charlotte said?

GJ: "'You have been my best friend,' replied Charlotte. 'That in itself is a tremendous thing.'"

ANGUS: Excellent. Now we've gotta stop at the courthouse.

GJ: But we wuz gonna merry-go-round. You broke yer promise.

ANGUS: I'm adding one postponement.

GJ: What's a post, post—

ANGUS: —A small delay. Sit on this bench, and I'll get you a cone of chocolate marshmallow.

(GJ immediately sits and purses his lips firmly shut)

ANGUS: If you don't say a word, I'll get you a double scoop.

GJ: I like—

ANGUS: —Sssh. Not a word.

(Estelle walks into scene)

ESTELLE: Well Angus Fletcher. I declare.

AGNUS: Miss Estelle. How's your rose empire flourishing?

ESTELLE: Added Wyoming. Estelle's Roses ships to thirty-two states. Master Gilbert Junior? Mighty quiet over there. Never known the cat to grab yer tongue.

ANGUS: He's practicing being quiet.

ESTELLE: Quiet is a stellar character builder. What on earth brings you brothers down to the courthouse?

ANGUS: I'm initiating a petition.

ESTELLE: Now I've heard everything. What magnitude of petition might you be "initiating?"

(ANGUS holds up the large envelope)

ANGUS: It's about street vendors.

ESTELLE: I already have a proposal before our city council.

ANGUS: Your proposal makes it illegal for vendors to sell on Brine Street. My petition makes it legal.

ESTELLE: Son, it ain't proper for a young man from Daugherty's prominent family to associate with trashy street vendors.

ANGUS: They add color, a touch of humanity to Brine Street. And tasty food.

ESTELLE: That disgusting animal slop is a health risk. I saw a Mexican out there stuffing who knows what into those round bread things.

ANGUS: *(Mumbling)* Tortillas—

ESTELLE: —Holding those bread things with her unclean hands.

ANGUS: Did you taste a tortilla?

ESTELLE: I value my life. Vendors invite disease and crime.

ANGUS: Have any been arrested?

ESTELLE: With my proposal, if they peddle that slop, they'll be arrested.

ANGUS: Talk with the vendors.

ESTELLE: I don't talk to Mexicans. Or Indians or Slavs. Whatever them gypsy sorts is.

ANGUS: Two minutes.

ESTELLE: I will not waste two minutes engaging in ignorant, criminal jibber jabber.

ANGUS: I'll stop jibber jabbering now and save you time to jibber jabber with the vendors.

ESTELLE: If your Granddaddy Daugherty was alive to hear you insult a city elder.

ANGUS: He'd be proud.

ESTELLE: Lowell Daugherty would feel sick to his stomach. No one will sign your impotent petition. Now, I have reasonable conversations to commence. Good day, Angus. Good day, Master GJ.

(She exits)

ANGUS: You can talk now.

(GJ has a questioning look and shrugs)

ANGUS: I said you can talk.

GJ: You wuz impolite. You made Miss Estelle severe mad.

ANGUS: She's racist, makes me mad.

GJ: Miss Estelle calls me, "Master." I like her. She's sweet.

ANGUS: Sweet? She has a bear hanging over her bedroom fireplace. Alaskan Grizzly. Bears that eat people. Miss Estelle took it down with one shot.

GJ: The bear tried to eat Miss Estelle?

ANGUS: Bears are no match against Southern women toting guns. Don't let her sweet-smelling roses fool you.

GJ: I won't, Angus. I like being called, "Master."

ANGUS: Stay here, "Master." I'll be back in five minutes.

GJ: I'm a master I'm a master.

(ANGUS exits)

End of Scene

DAUGHERTY PARK MERRY-GO-ROUND

ACT ONE

SCENE TWO

Setting: Brine Street Food Cart. Day. ANGUS and GJ walk toward a food cart attended by JAMES and SHANNON. GJ is chewing on an empty ice-cream cone.

GJ: I'm out.

ANGUS: Cause you inhaled those two scoops of chocolate marshmallow. Wonder you don't throw up.

JAMES: Hi. Anything we can do for you two? Oh! Shannon? This is that smart guy I told you about who started that petition.

SHANNON: Oh, so nice to meet you guys. I'm Shannon. James told me how helpful you are. Nice to meet yous.

ANGUS: Nice to meet you too. I'm Angus.

JAMES: Angus! I knew it was some royalty kinda name.

SHANNON: Angus. That's a new one. I have never heard somebody called, "Angus."

GJ: It's a breed of cow.

ANGUS: This is my brother GJ.

SHANNON: Well, GJ, looks like you loved your ice-cream cone to death, baby doll. Wore the ice cream right out of that little cone.

GJ: I inhaled it.

SHANNON: That's so cute. Do you like southwest food?

GJ: Do I Angus?

ANGUS: You like Taco Bell.

GJ: Are we going to Taco Bell?

ANGUS: I'm sure this is tastier.

GJ: I like Taco Bell.

ANGUS: Can you make him something not spicy?

GJ: I spit out spicy.

ANGUS: He does.

JAMES: One not spicy soft taco coming up.

SHANNON: People down South are so nice. I feel bad imposing on you, inconveniencing you.

ANGUS: What inconvenience?

SHANNON: Causing you to bother all your friends to sign a petition, trudge all over town in this hot sun.

ANGUS: No bother, really.

SHANNON: Nice people always say, "No bother." But I know it is.

JAMES: Here you go, big guy.

GJ: That ain't Taco Bell.

ANGUS: Say, "thank you." If you don't like it, I'll eat it.

(He hands money to JAMES)

GJ: Thank you, sir.

(He tastes taco, makes a sour face, rapidly flaps hand)

SHANNON: Too spicy, honey?

(GJ shakes head, strains to talk, and coughs)

GJ: I swallowed my Juicy Fruit.

ANGUS: You were chewing gum while eating ice cream?

SHANNON: That's so cute. Freezes the gum up hard. I do that all the time.

JAMES: You need water. Swig this down, big fellow.

(He hands cup to GJ, who gulps water and then breathes with relief)

GJ: Ah.

ANGUS: What do you say?

GJ: Thank you for that nice cup of water, sir. It was fine water.

JAMES: Fancy manners.

SHANNON: So polite, GJ.

GJ: See Angus.

ANGUS: I see.

GJ: Can you finish this west food for me?

ANGUS: Southwest.

GJ: Can you?

ANGUS: When we get home.

JAMES: Here's a bag.

ANGUS: Thank you. I should get him home. Pleasure to meet both of you.

SHANNON: The pleasure was all ours.

GJ: You have nice hair, lady.

ANGUS: Bye James. And uh ... uh ...

SHANNON: Shannon.

ANGUS: Shannon. Good day.

(GJ flaps his hands with excitement)

GJ: Bye lady!

(ANGUS and GJ exit)

JAMES: Knew that dude would notch up your thermostat.

SHANNON: Felt chilly to me. And that other one?

JAMES: A retard.

SHANNON: Who'd guess those brothers are worth squat?

JAMES: Millions.

SHANNON: Think he liked me?

(JAMES imitates GJ's voice and flaps his hands)

JAMES: "Bye lady, you have nice hair."

SHANNON: Not him!

JAMES: You came on strong enough to scare that guy off.

SHANNON: What the hell kinda name is "Angus?" At first, I thought he said, "Agnes."

JAMES: Call him "Agnes" and our plans are shit.

SHANNON: Just cause I play dumb—

JAMES: *(Imitating SHANNON)*—"Don't mean I am dumb."

(SHANNON pouts)

JAMES: Oh. She has on her pouty face.

(He kisses SHANNON passionately; she returns kiss, but then pulls away)

SHANNON: Someone could see us, asshole. Let's clear the hell outta here.

(They pack the cart and exit)

End of Scene

DAUGHERTY PARK MERRY-GO-ROUND

ACT ONE
SCENE THREE

Setting: Daugherty Park near pond. Night. SHANNON and ANGUS are sitting on a picnic blanket.

(Audio: Crickets softly chirping)

ANGUS: I was four when Long Neck died. He became my first box-turtle shell. I found another shell, and my turtle shell collection was up and away.

SHANNON: What's GJ collect?

ANGUS: Spiders. Dozens of 'em.

SHANNON: Oooh. Jimmy—I mean James—is allergic to spiders. Swears his heart'll stop instantly.

ANGUS: Lots of spiders in Daugherty Park.

(SHANNON surveys environment, moves closer to ANGUS. ANGUS slaps the palm of his hand on the ground.)

ANGUS: Got one!

SHANNON: Mother of ...

(ANGUS laughs, opens his empty hand. SHANNON playfully slaps him.)

SHANNON: That's mean.

(ANGUS frowns at being hit)

ANGUS: *(Pause)* Our last hint of sun.

SHANNON: It's a beautiful, pink ... what? Pink shining off the pond?

ANGUS: Uh … shining, bouncing, shimmering, sparkling, dancing … Shining's good. Fireworks go off in an hour.

SHANNON: I love fireworks! Especially purple. And green. Purple and green together.

ANGUS: I feel like a little kid every time.

SHANNON: Ooooh. Aaaaah. Ooooh. Aaaah.

ANGUS: I do that.

SHANNON: So, Daugherty Park's named after your family?

ANGUS: My mom's side. Who told you that?

SHANNON: GJ.

ANGUS: When did you see him?

SHANNON: He dropped by with a group of people from a school or something.

ANGUS: Sheltered workshop. Avery School.

SHANNON: Yeah that. He described your family.

ANGUS: I would hate to hear my brother describe our family.

SHANNON: It was sweet.

ANGUS: Our family tree is not what I'd call, "sweet."

SHANNON: He said your mother died in a car accident.

ANGUS: Car accident?

(SHANNON nods)

ANGUS: Well, it was in a car. But not the way people think of car accidents. Mom suffocated in her Lincoln.

SHANNON: Oh my.

ANGUS: Carbon monoxide. Asphyxiated.

SHANNON: That's horrifying.

ANGUS: Over there. That little dirt maintenance road. Mom and Clifford Moore.

SHANNON: What happened?

ANGUS: People around here invent and reinvent myths. They say, those people say, Mom and Clifford Moore were making out.

SHANNON: People are cruel.

ANGUS: That they are.

SHANNON: Cause she was having an affair?—You don't have to spill your guts out if it hurts too much.

ANGUS: *(Pause)* Clifford Moore was fifteen-years old.

SHANNON: Fifteen?

ANGUS: Mom wasn't … fifteen.

(ANGUS plays with a stick, draws lines in the dirt by his foot. SHANNON watches for a moment.)

SHANNON: My mom was thirteen when she dropped me into this world. Whoever the dope was who … He sure wasn't thirteen.

(Long, awkward pause)

ANGUS: *(Sarcastic)* This is a fun picnic.

(SHANNON stares at ANGUS, breaks into laughter. ANGUS is puzzled, breaks into laughter. They fall back onto the blanket. Laugher subsides.)

ANGUS: See that star up there? Between that fork in the top branches?

(SHANNON points toward the sky)

SHANNON: There?

ANGUS: No, just a little bit …

(He takes SHANNON'S arm and moves it a small amount)

ANGUS: Right there.

SHANNON: Oh, yeah.

ANGUS: That's my lucky star. Mom said it was her gift to me … Told me to never let go of it.

SHANNON: You still got it.

ANGUS: When the sky is clear.

SHANNON: She musta been a terrific mom.

ANGUS: Yeah ... She used to read *Charlotte's Web* to GJ. The two of them would laugh so exuberantly it was contagious. Good times.

(He sits up)

ANGUS: Did you have good times with your mother?

(SHANNON sits up)

SHANNON: You can kiss me if you want.

ANGUS: Uh … Sure ... I guess.

(He half-heartedly kisses SHANNON. She pulls away.)

SHANNON: I shouldn't have asked you to kiss me. Now I feel bad.

ANGUS: No, it's fine. I just … It's fine.

SHANNON: You probably got somebody.

ANGUS: No.

SHANNON: That's good. I mean, it'd be bad if I made you cheat, you know.

ANGUS: Sure … But golly that was fast.

SHANNON: I like you lots.

ANGUS: You seem nice.

SHANNON: Am I too simple … not the caliber of person you would … you know?

ANGUS: Nice is what matters.

SHANNON: Maybe since you come from money and all. I don't.

ANGUS: I come from money? Who says?

SHANNON: GJ.

ANGUS: GJ? Five dollars to GJ is: "coming from money."

SHANNON: He said he had millions.

ANGUS: Millions? ... Well ... We have trust funds. When we turn 26, or marry. So theoretically ... I put off college. Started an organic farm. Supply restaurants that are into organic. Build my own restaurant someday, cook with food I grow.

SHANNON: I am so particular about what I put into my body. You read about fast-food places and junk ... Our bodies are like you know: sacred.

ANGUS: I try to teach that to GJ but ... ice cream rules.

SHANNON: He said your grandfather died in a plane crash.

ANGUS: He said that? Huh ... Small plane. Flying to Raleigh. State Democratic meeting. Plane blew up. Broke my grandma's heart. She died soon after.

SHANNON: Lost your mother. Lost your grandparents. So, trust funds.

ANGUS: *(Pause)* GJ is a real blabber mouth, huh?

SHANNON: You got a father?

ANGUS: Oh yeah. Lives across this pond, over that hill. A recluse. When our grandma gave it to him, it was a farm. But he never farmed it. He sits ... drinks ... reads conspiracy theories, shoots guns on a little range he built. Blasts away logs, coffee cans, whiskey bottles.

SHANNON: You and GJ. Two guys alone in this world.

ANGUS: Feels that way.

SHANNON: Me and my brother. Same. Alone.

ANGUS: James is your brother?

SHANNON: Who the fuck did you think he was?

ANGUS: Your, well that you two are together.

SHANNON: Hell no. That's so funny. I wouldn't be asking guys to kiss me if … No way.

(She pauses, massages ANGUS'S shoulders. ANGUS becomes uncomfortable.)

ANGUS: I should check on my brother. He gets into mischief fast.

SHANNON: What about the fireworks?

ANGUS: Let's not use up all our fun in one thrill-packed evening.

SHANNON: Angus? It's swell getting to know you.

ANGUS: Sorry I hogged the story sharing.

SHANNON: I got to meet your family … through your eyes.

ANGUS: Yes, well … We'll run into one another again.

SHANNON: Soon?

ANGUS: *(Half-hearted)* Sure.

(He pops up)

ANGUS: Ready?

SHANNON: Uh … Guess so.

(ANGUS pulls SHANNON to her feet)

ANGUS: There you go, Miss.

(He folds the blanket)

SHANNON: I do like that star. Your star.

(ANGUS nods, packs the blanket into the basket, walks away. SHANNON watches as ANGUS walks away, and then follows.)

End of Scene

DAUGHERTY PARK MERRY-GO-ROUND

ACT ONE

SCENE FOUR

Setting: Gil's small farmhouse. Day. There are numerous pickle jars on the table. GIL is feeding pickle bits on toothpicks to ANGUS.

GIL: Okay, close your eyes. Open your mouth. What's this taste like?

ANGUS: *(Following all of GIL'S orders)* Dill pickle.

GIL: Right. Rinse with water ... Spit in the pail. Okay, close your eyes. Mouth open. What's this taste like?

ANGUS: Bread and butter.

GIL: Excellent. Rinse ... Spit. Close. Open. And this?

ANGUS: Sweet midget.

GIL: Good. Look on the table. What do you see?

ANGUS: Pickle jars.

GIL: Do better than that.

ANGUS: Dill, bread and butter, sweet midget pickle jars.

GIL: Andy Warhol looked at Campbell's Soup cans and saw art.

ANGUS: Andy Warhol was a genius artist. I come from a family of pickle canners.

GIL: Don't short shrift yerself, boy.

ANGUS: I don't, uh ... variety. Varieties of pickles.

GIL: Pickles vary.

ANGUS: They do vary.

GIL: Like wines.

ANGUS: Like wines? *(Laughing)* Pickles vary like wines?

GIL: Listen to me ... Listen to me ... How do wines start?

ANGUS: Grapes?

GIL: How do pickles start?

ANGUS: Cucumbers?

GIL: Elements in the soil alter delicate tastes. Nitrates. Phosphates. Dry growing seasons, wet growing seasons. Cultivated grapes. Cultivated cucumbers. Altering refined qualities. Some match perfectly with specific foods, others with other foods.

ANGUS: Let's see maître de, bring me Marlborough Sauvignon Blanc 97 and Daugherty sweet midgets 2010.

GIL: Listen! ... Chop 'em up and you have relish.

ANGUS: Add eggs and mayo and voilà: egg salad.

GIL: Listen! ... The big picture is this ... *(Choking up)* the big picture is ...

ANGUS: Big picture.

GIL: Look ... beyond ... the jar.

ANGUS: *(Baffled pause)* Beyond the jar?

GIL: *(Still choked up)* Beyond. Something else, isn't it?

ANGUS: It is ... something else.

GIL: *(Crying)* So few people grasp that.

ANGUS: I'm glad you ... shared.

GIL: I've waited for this father-son connection ever since your mom died. That horrible, horny Clifford boy seducing her.

ANGUS: Feel better now?

GIL: *(Struggling to compose)* One day, as a dad, you'll discover the pride I feel this moment.

ANGUS: I'm glad you feel ... this moment.

GIL: You ever ponder, lie awake at night asking yourself why I got fired from Daugherty Pickles?

ANGUS: Not really.

GIL: Those same assholes that did in John Fitzgerald Kennedy.

ANGUS: Oswald?

GIL: Cubans.

ANGUS: Ah. Cubans.

GIL: I talked Daugherty Pickles into making relish. Relish needs sugar. Sugar cane is grown in Cuba. Kennedy set up a Cuban embargo and an outright attack, Bay of Pigs.

ANGUS: Were you even born then?

GIL: Look ... beyond the jar.

ANGUS: Yes sir.

GIL: Well ... enough about life philosophy. What did you want to talk to me about?

ANGUS: Oh right, uh, nothing philosophical, profound.

GIL: When sons request talks with fathers, those moments are profound. Shoot.

ANGUS: Okay ... When you met Mom, first started dating ...

GIL: Wondered when you'd ask my advice on the women. Shoot.

ANGUS: What feelings did you notice toward Mom?

GIL: Feelings I never had before. There's something hooked up between trust and love up here. *(Pointing to brain)* And what happens down here between the legs. Fullness. Excitement. Feeling wet. That's all I'm gonna say about that.

ANGUS: That was plenty.

GIL: We met at Duke. Louise always thought she only got into Duke cause her dad and granddad donated a hospital wing. Up til the day she died, she never accepted how bright she was. Always asking, “Do you think I’m simple?” And there she was, the most sophisticated, brightest, sparkling human ever. That stirred up feelings here in my chest. Like I was floating. If someone blew air in my face, I would have floated off like a kid’s carnival balloon.

ANGUS: Light.

GIL: You got anybody like that?

ANGUS: I meet people, here and there, experience a whisper of what you describe.

GIL: Reason we’re on this planet. Search for it. When you find it? Grab it completely. *(Pause)* Now close your eyes and open your mouth. I got another pickle.

End of Scene

DAUGHERTY PARK MERRY-GO-ROUND

ACT ONE

SCENE FIVE

Setting: Brine Street food cart. Day. JAMES, wearing an apron, holds up a taco as ESTELLE walks past.

JAMES: Soft or hard, ma'am? I'm sure to satisfy you.

(ESTELLE glares at JAMES and exits)

JAMES: No taco for the whacko.

(SHANNON enters, pouts)

JAMES: Ain't happy to see me? No. Don't tell me you and money boy struck out again.

SHANNON: He's not interested in me, Jimmy. Four times. Nothing!

JAMES: You drag him to fuckin' girlie movies. This guy's the action type.

SHANNON: I think your "action-type guy" don't like women.

JAMES: He just don't like YOU.

SHANNON: I tried to rodeo ride him.

JAMES: No details!

SHANNON: Rodeo him! Top and bottom! Angus is queer. Angus just don't know Angus is queer.

JAMES: This sucks. Fuck! We gotta make a plan B.

SHANNON: A plan B? I'll give you a plan B. YOU take your action buddy's little ass to an all-action movie.

JAMES: Shit no!!! No trust fund is ... Hell no.

SHANNON: Millions, Jimmy. Millions.

JAMES: A plan C! ... You take GJ, the retardo's ass, to a movie.

SHANNON: You've been hitting the stuff again.

(She mimes snorting cocaine)

JAMES: Not for six months ... Two months.

SHANNON: So what? You suddenly went stupid on me?

JAMES: Watch your mouth.

SHANNON: It's okay I pony up as a whore for plan A, plans X, Y, Z. I bring in money doing the nasty. What do you do? You sit. Look charming and talk, talk, talk.

JAMES: I'm the executive decision maker.

SHANNON: What about I be the executive decision maker on account'a your executive decision-making SUCKS? You do the big nasty. Or did you snort so much you can't get it up again?

JAMES: Watch your mouth.

SHANNON: Or what? You'll gamble away our money? Oh, that's right. You already did that.

JAMES: I had a bad streak.

SHANNON: Three bad streaks.

JAMES: Ssssh. Here comes your "nasty."

SHANNON: I'm telling you, gangster guy, Angus wants your sweet tight ass.

(ANGUS enters and quick steps to the cart)

ANGUS: *(Enthusiastic)* Hi James! *(Less enthusiastic)* Shannon.

SHANNON: Angus.

ANGUS: Good day to be outdoors.

SHANNON: Fantastic day to be outdoors. Sunny, hot, oh so hot. And you know what? Jimmy, James was just talking about you. Angus this, Angus that.

ANGUS: Yeah?

SHANNON: I had told him what you told me about swimming in that rock quarry thing outside'a town. Skinny dipping? James is too bashful to tell you, but he's big time into swimming au naturel. Him and his muscular man friends camping down on the Gulf.

ANGUS: Gulf of Mexico?

SHANNON: Florida or Kentucky island somewhere. Nude beach. So nude. James won't never ask you, but, he's dying to get away from me; I'm driving him fucking crazy. He needs to kick off his shoes with a man friend … Play around.

JAMES: I'm fine here.

SHANNON: Go swim with your buddy Angus. The two of yous, like you was wishing for.

ANGUS: It is hot today.

SHANNON: So hot!

JAMES: I don't have trunks.

SHANNON: Trunks? Just the two a'you. You up for swimming, Angus?

ANGUS: A swim could be nice.

SHANNON: Settled. I watch the cart. Easy as cake, easy as pie, whichever's easy. You two deserve time without me around dramatizing.

ANGUS: I was heading to the farm to check my tomatoes, string up fish line to freak deer away.

SHANNON: James loves gardening.

ANGUS: Farming.

SHANNON: Farming even more. Wait til you see him swim. Regular Olympian. Firm abs. Awesome biceps. You two tough and tumble men get off and play. Scoot, skedaddle.

JAMES: *(To SHANNON)* I will remember this … Sister.

SHANNON: Sweet brother. Ain't he sweet, Angus?

(ANGUS shrugs. SHANNON jerks apron off of JAMES and puts it on herself.)

SHANNON: Don't mind the time, guys. Me in my little kitchen in the great of outdoors. If nature moves you, stay all night.

JAMES: I will remember.

SHANNON: Get off on nature, you two hunks. Love ya bro. You too, Angus.

(She tosses kisses to them. ANGUS and JAMES exit.)

SHANNON: I like plan B. *(Singing)* "Whistle while you work, da da da da. Whistle while you work."

End of Scene

DAUGHERTY PARK MERRY-GO-ROUND

ACT ONE
SCENE SIX

Setting: Brine Street food cart. Day. One week later. SHANNON, sitting by food cart, is painting her toenails. GJ enters, sluggishly walks to cart.

GJ: Hi lady.

SHANNON: GJ! How are you, baby doll? Where you been all week? I miss you.

GJ: I forget your name.

SHANNON: That's all right, sugar. It's Shannon.

GJ: I thought that name, but I don't wanna be wrong. Shannon. Pretty name like Dannon. My yogurt.

SHANNON: Dannon. Good way to remember it. Shannon, Dannon.

GJ: I claw-grabbed you something.

SHANNON: Claw-grabbed?

GJ: I brung you this teddy whale on account'a I couldn't claw-grab the teddy bear. I run out of quarters.

SHANNON: Well, I like this "teddy whale" even better.

(GJ flaps his hands with excitement)

GJ: I like you like it.

SHANNON: I will carry this cute little whale everywhere I go.

GJ: I like you.

SHANNON: Well, I like you too, GJ. Did you come here all by yourself?

GJ: I brung myself cuz Angus run off.

SHANNON: He's with James. They swim afternoons.

GJ: Oh … I can't swim none.

SHANNON: Me neither. Me and you? We're the same.

GJ: Is Angus mad at me?

SHANNON: Angus loves you. Talks about you non-stop.

GJ: He don't bring me nowhere no more.

SHANNON: He's not mad at you. He needs time to be with his friend James. And James needs his friend Angus.

GJ: Is Angus your friend too?

SHANNON: Didn't exactly go that direction.

GJ: He told me you are nice and should be "permitted" on Brine Street.

SHANNON: How sweet. And sweet you came all this way to see me.

GJ: Angus learned me to find my way to Brine Street.

SHANNON: GJ honey? Angus TAUGHT you how to find your way to Brine Street, not learned you.

GJ: I can't never figure them words out.

SHANNON: Listen sweetie, you do not learn someone, you teach someone. Someone does not learn you, someone teaches you.

GJ: I hate them words.

SHANNON: Try this, I teach you; you learn … I teach you; you learn. Say that back to me. I teach you.

GJ: I teach you.

SHANNON: You learn.

GJ: You learn.

SHANNON: You teach me; I learn.

GJ: You teach me; I learn.

SHANNON: Perfect. Now, I teach you ... and?

GJ: ... I learn?

SHANNON: You teach me ... and?

GJ: ... You learn?

SHANNON: One hundred percent correct. So good!

GJ: I teach you and you learn. You teach me and I learn.

SHANNON: You got it!

(GJ flaps his hands with excitement)

GJ: I learned it. I learned it.

SHANNON: You did learn it.

GJ: You taught me. I learned it.

SHANNON: So good, GJ.

GJ: That ain't hard.

SHANNON: It's hard but you learned it.

GJ: Cuz you splained it good. Angus never splained me.

SHANNON: You are a bona fide learner, GJ.

GJ: I learned ... cause you teached, I mean taught. Shoot, I done it wrong.

(GJ repetitively slaps the top of his head)

SHANNON: No, no! Only a little bit wrong, honey.

(After a moment, GJ calms)

GJ: Thank you Dannon—I mean Shannon.

SHANNON: You are welcome, GJ. Do you want something to eat, baby doll?

GJ: No thank you, ma'am, I tasted that last week ... I mean, no thank you ma'am. Next time I visit I might could ... ma'am.

SHANNON: Some water?

GJ: Yes, please. I come the long way by accident, and I am so thirsty. Thank you, ma'am. You are a very nice lady, and I like your good water.

SHANNON: And you are very nice, GJ. A nice GENTLEMAN.

(GJ flaps his hands with excitement)

GJ: Lady and gentleman!

SHANNON: Lady and gentleman.

End of Scene

DAUGHERTY PARK MERRY-GO-ROUND

ACT ONE

SCENE SEVEN

Setting: Daugherty Park near pond. Night. ANGUS and JAMES are wrapped in towels, lying on a blanket.

(Audio: Crickets chirping)

ANGUS: We've never stayed this late after swimming. Night sneaked up fast. Crickets. Lightning bugs.

JAMES: A good day, Angus. Yep.

ANGUS: Yep.

JAMES: I wish I swam like you. You're a super porpoise. I dog paddle.

ANGUS: I like watching you swim. You have energy. Everything you do. *(Pause)* I sure like this park.

JAMES: Cause your family donated it?

ANGUS: I have good memories here. One over there ... and one over there ... and another there ...

JAMES: I like visiting your park.

ANGUS: I like sharing this park with you.

JAMES: Don't tell anyone I said that, okay?

ANGUS: Said what?

JAMES: That I like to come out here with you. People get strange ideas. I just meant it's cool to get out of town.

ANGUS: People have stupid ideas. I don't care anymore.

JAMES: You're always nice to me.

ANGUS: You're nice to me. *(Pause)* See that star up there? Between the forks in the top branches?

(JAMES points at sky)

JAMES: There?

(ANGUS moves JAMES'S arm with his hand and continues to hold onto it)

ANGUS: There. That star ... It's my gift to you. Whenever you look up at that star, remember it's from me.

(JAMES quickly retracts his arm)

JAMES: That's like shit a guy says to a girl.

ANGUS: My mom gave me that star. I think of her when I see it. Sorry. You don't have to share it if you don't want.

JAMES: No, it's ... Nobody ever gave me no star before.

ANGUS: I never shared my star before.

JAMES: You are one unusual human being, Angus Fletcher.

ANGUS: I don't want to be unusual.

JAMES: Good unusual. You care what people feel, what people think ... Fucks up my mind.

(ANGUS sits motionless)

JAMES: A couple of days back, when we was drunk at the rock quarry?

ANGUS: My head still aches.

JAMES: And we fell asleep, side by side?

ANGUS: I got sunburned.

JAMES: I was scared you would ... Nothing.

ANGUS: Golly, James. I would never ... I don't want ... anything.

JAMES: *(Pause)* You've never had sex with anyone, have you? Woman or man?

ANGUS: That obvious, huh? *(Sighs)* ... I'm waiting.

JAMES: People think I'm some kind of whoremonger. I ain't.

ANGUS: You don't chase after—

JAMES: —Course I do. Not that fuckin' much. More than fuckin' you of course.

ANGUS: Of course.

JAMES: I start lots ... I don't hardly finish. Sucks.

ANGUS: Wow.

JAMES: But you're totally waiting. That sucks more.

ANGUS: I don't mind.

JAMES: What the shit?

ANGUS: I want to know for sure, absolutely know. Not just ... I need to know.

JAMES: What the hell's there to know?

ANGUS: Know my heart, know the person I love's heart ... know we both ...

JAMES: ... Both what?

ANGUS: ... Feel safe.

JAMES: You break my heart Angus ... Nobody ever broke my heart like you do.

ANGUS: *(Pause)* That's the nicest thing anybody ever said to me.

(JAMES looks away and stares at sky. ANGUS stares at JAMES and then stares at his feet.)

JAMES: *(After a moment)* Shooting star.

(They both stare at the sky)

End of Scene

DAUGHERTY PARK MERRY-GO-ROUND

ACT ONE

SCENE EIGHT

Setting: Gil's small farm house. GIL is intensely reading a magazine with a magnifying glass. ANGUS leans in through the door.

ANGUS: Dad?

GIL: Angus. Studying how these young fellows execute drone strikes. Young child men with their hands on joy sticks. Hard to sleep knowing such things rule. What's on your mind? More woman worries?

ANGUS: Not really.

GIL: Street vendor troubles?

ANGUS: What makes you say that?

GIL: Estelle informed me of your petition.

ANGUS: Estelle.

GIL: And GJ brought it up. Called it, "a partition."

ANGUS: He understood about my petition?

GIL: He said you wrote "a partition" that insulted Estelle way more than he insulted Aunt Phoebe's velvet cake. I put two and two together; you can envision the rest.

ANGUS: Probably not, but yes, a "petition" to allow, encourage street vendors on Brine Street.

GIL: Also said you sleep with a street vendor.

ANGUS: Pardon?

GIL: You sleep with a street vendor.

ANGUS: *(Pause)* Did he say which street vendor?

GIL: How many street vendors do you sleep with?

ANGUS: In GJ's mind?

GIL: With your body.

ANGUS: GJ and I met a brother and sister who are street vendors. Did he say which—

GIL: —Jimmy.

ANGUS: Jimmy? James. Let me get this straight. GJ said I sleep with the brother, not the sister?

GIL: He said he sleeps with the sister, and you sleep with the brother.

ANGUS: GJ sleeps with Shannon?

GIL: In a simple fashion I imagine.

ANGUS: I don't wanna imagine.

GIL: And you sleep with James.

ANGUS: Slept. We only slept. In Daugherty Park.

GIL: You and James?

ANGUS: We drank, passed out … Slept.

GIL: Uh huh.

ANGUS: Don't read something into it that's not there. When did you see GJ?

GIL: He dropped by this morning.

ANGUS: Before noon?

GIL: Whining you won't give him quarters for the "claw-grab" machine. He wants to "claw-grab" a ring from the machine at Walt and Merv's Pool Hall so he can get married.

ANGUS: Married??? He's proposing???

GIL: What do you know about his woman? Who GJ said you slept with before you drunkenly slept beside her brother.

ANGUS: I didn't sleep ... She likes Mexican food, Czech garlic-laced food, some Ethiopian, hates British. Addicted to Ho Ho Cakes. Travels a lot.

GIL: With carnivals.

ANGUS: And circuses.

GIL: GJ said she likes merry-go-rounds and tilt-a-whirls.

ANGUS: Rodeos too.

GIL: Said she teaches him bedroom games.

ANGUS: Oh my God!

GIL: He sleeps with the sister, and you sleep with the brother. Pardon me, beside the brother. My question is this ...

ANGUS: Yes sir?

GIL: Are you a homosexual?

ANGUS: No. No sir. I am not.

GIL: Uh huh ... Maybe. Maybe not. I should never have allowed your mother to name you, "Angus."

ANGUS: Why did she name me, "Angus?"

GIL: After GJ was born, being simple like he is, your mother blamed my Fletcher genetics for corrupting her refined Daugherty genetics. So, she went on a nine-day fling with a North Carolina State exchange student. An Aussie named, "Angus Winslow."

ANGUS: You're not my biological father?

GIL: How do you feel about that?

ANGUS: Uh, mixed, mixed emotions, sir ... Australian?

GIL: Queer as a seven-dollar bill.

ANGUS: Three-dollar bill. Why do you think that?

GIL: His middle name was "Shirley."

ANGUS: That's a common British male name.

GIL: When I say J. Edgar Hoover and Angus Shirley Winslow were both queer; it's truth.

ANGUS: No reason to try to follow that logic.

GIL: Now son, you may possibly be homosexual, I won't rush to judgment, but in my heart of hearts, it's imperative you're not queer.

ANGUS: The difference?

GIL: What's the difference between a soldier and a mercenary? A dog and a wolf? A Republican and a Tea Partier? The big picture?

ANGUS: Beyond the jar?

GIL: Exactly! Now this woman GJ sleeps with, wants to marry, between you and me, I cannot picture GJ knows … How to say this … Knows where to stick it in.

ANGUS: I can't picture he knows what to stick in.

GIL: I asked him about these bedroom games. He said she played games with Mr. Mickey.

ANGUS: Mr. Mickey?

GIL: As a boy he called it his "weenie doggie." Not sure why he renamed it.

ANGUS: Last year at a cookout, Freddy Yates pointed at hot dogs blistering on the grill and screamed, "die fat little weenie doggies."

GIL: How much do you like this Jimmy fella?

ANGUS: James.

GIL: James.

ANGUS: He's … interesting.

GIL: Estelle says he's a carnie.

ANGUS: Street vendor.

GIL: Are you going to go to college like we discussed, or are you hell bent on spending the rest of your life shacking up with carnie street vendors?

ANGUS: You know I can't go to college. GJ depends on me day and night.

GIL: GJ will be fine.

ANGUS: He won't be fine. Look what's happening now. Shannon is a slick, scary manipulator.

GIL: A woman.

ANGUS: She's after his trust money.

GIL: I concur, but hell, if she'll take GJ, let's sweeten his pot'a gold and wish 'em well. Hells bells.

ANGUS: Throw him under the bus?

GIL: Focus on what you need. This brother-sister team is rotten. The sister wants to marry a retard; the brother shacks up with a turtle-shell collector.

ANGUS: I'm an organic farmer.

GIL: Be capable of seeing the big view. The sister will marry GJ, then the brother'll knock you off.

ANGUS: He would never hurt me.

GIL: Then knock off GJ and BAM! This evil pair has sixteen million dollars.

ANGUS: I know you believe your conspiracies.

GIL: Estelle dug up a report. These two are wanted in Tennessee and Louisiana. The "sister" married two men in their late 80s. Both died suspicious deaths.

ANGUS: How suspicious?

GIL: One choked on an over-sized chocolate-dipped New Zealand strawberry. One drowned on his knees in the kitchen, face down in rock-salt water of his ice-cream maker.

ANGUS: Oh my gosh! James gave me an ice-cream maker as a friendship gift. A used ice-cream maker.

GIL: There you go.

ANGUS: This cannot be happening.

GIL: You're bright. I know you see what has to be done.

ANGUS: We've got to confront them. Turn them in. At least scare them away.

GIL: Kill them.

ANGUS: Kill them??? Earth to Dad. Come in, Dad.

GIL: You know I'm right.

ANGUS: What's right is to contact the authorities.

GIL: For playing with Mr. Mickey and whatever you call yours?

ANGUS: Adam.

GIL: Adam?

ANGUS: Adam Anteater. Boys in gym class teased me mine was shaped like an ...

GIL: Your mom's idea to not circumcise you. So, you would look like her Aussie hottie.

ANGUS: The hits keep coming. *(Pause)* You said James and Shannon are wanted in two states?

GIL: More under other aliases.

ANGUS: You listen to me for once. This is our plan: you tell Estelle; I'll tell Sheriff Conklin. Above board, perfectly legal, soundly sane.

GIL: Sane as God-damn fairy dust. Grow a spine, boy. Be a he-man amongst your kind.

ANGUS: My kind? What kind is that? Someone who can't figure out how to be sexual? Not be a killer?

GIL: Calm down. Put this crisis in perspective.

ANGUS: Killing two people doesn't fit into perspective.

GIL: Now YOU listen to me! There's stupid killing, there's evil killing, there's vengeful killing, there's drunken killing, there's horny killing—

ANGUS: —My gosh.

GIL: And then there's poetic, creative, iconic execution.

ANGUS: You've given this a scary amount of thought.

(GIL points to his head)

GIL: I realize it's a stretch for you to leap from pickle jar talk to timed-explosives talk.

ANGUS: Timed what???

GIL: Estelle uses explosives to scare off crows.

ANGUS: Explosives?

GIL: Word travels crow to crow.

ANGUS: Dad, Dad, Dad, if that were true, I would have heard explosions.

GIL: She times her little fertilizer bombs to go off when pickle trains rattle through town.

ANGUS: Wait a minute … Last spring that old farmer up on Horton's Ridge. His tractor blew up.

GIL: You'll have to ask Estelle about that.

ANGUS: Oh my gosh, oh my gosh, oh my gosh!

GIL: What?

ANGUS: On the way to his Raleigh Democratic meeting, Grandfather Daugherty's plane blew up.

GIL: You'll have to ask Republicans about that.

ANGUS: What kind of town is this?

GIL: Like any town, cept we can pickles.

ANGUS: This morning, I woke up in James's arms, feeling safe, the most content I felt in all my life.

GIL: In a fella's arms.

ANGUS: Those floating feelings you talked about. Like a kid's balloon.

GIL: It'd be a stretch, but guess I might could envision that.

ANGUS: Good. Cause I no longer can envision happiness.

GIL: You're discombobulated. Love's an angry sickness.

ANGUS: I don't want anyone to hold me. I don't want anyone to sleep next to me. Not swim with me. Not talk to me, not touch me, not even be near me.

GIL: Don't be a drama queen.

ANGUS: I'm not!

GIL: You're whining like a pansy.

ANGUS: Stop calling me names!

GIL: I'm not. I'm labeling your behaviors.

ANGUS: What makes you an authority on homosexuality?

GIL: Your grandfather Daugherty.

ANGUS: No, no, no, no. I don't need to hear more.

(He walks toward door)

GIL: Where are you going? We have killings to plan.

ANGUS: Listen to what you're saying.

GIL: If you get emotional, you'll get sloppy. Sloppy killing's the lowest.

ANGUS: Choke James and Shannon on dill pickles. Pickle executions.

GIL: Go to college, Angus. Grow some problem-solving skills.

ANGUS: These are the problem-solving skills you learned at Duke?

GIL: National Guard.

ANGUS: I'm outta here.

GIL: Where you going?

ANGUS: To the park. Spin myself on the merry-go-round.

GIL: If that settles you, go spin. Then march back here as a responsible man and lead the plan on snuffin' out these two. I'll toss weenies on the grill.

ANGUS: You are insane, crazy, loony, paranoid, and you need to use deodorant.

GIL: You're calling me names.

ANGUS: I'm labeling your behaviors.

GIL: I am a heterosexual man. I absorb insults and still maintain focus. See? I'm calm. Saying this calmly, saying this sanely: we have vermin to exterminate.

ANGUS: When I was six years old, day and night I obsessed about running away. I blew it.

(He walks toward door)

GIL: Don't let people see you spinning on your merry-go-round. People'll think you're a batty boy.

ANGUS: A what???

GIL: Batty boy. Jamaican term. I apologize for calling you a label, but you crippled my self-worth. You said I smell bad.

ANGUS: I'm sorry, Dad. I take back ... Actually, I can't. You do smell bad.

(He walks toward door)

GIL: Wait! Come back here.

(He kneels)

ANGUS: Now what?

GIL: Get down here with me.

ANGUS: We're praying???

GIL: *(Gentle)* On yer knees, son.

(ANGUS sighs and reluctantly kneels)

GIL: Close your eyes.

(ANGUS sighs louder and closes eyes)

GIL: Dear God. Help me and my son to be thankful that you gave us power, gave us creativity to think, to imagine, that you gave us knowledge to learn who we are. Now … grant us the wisdom to not take actions based upon who we are, but actions based upon thy grand plan. Amen.

(ANGUS stands as GIL remains kneeling)

ANGUS: If your and God's grand plan is to execute people for being born stupid, I'll implement my own plan. Stay put. I'll contact the Sheriff and Estelle.

GIL: Tell Estelle for me, we need an extra-large order of roses.

ANGUS: Roses???

GIL: Color don't matter. But be sure to tell her, "EXTRA-large order."

ANGUS: Maybe I did violate God's laws. Cause I sure am in hell already being punished.

GIL: Tell her!!!

(ANGUS walks to door, stops and turns)

ANGUS: I'll pick up deodorant for you.

(He exits)

End of Scene

DAUGHERTY PARK MERRY-GO-ROUND

ACT ONE
SCENE NINE

Setting: Estelle's office. Day. ESTELLE, sitting at desk, is comparing two sets of papers. ANGUS leans in door.

ANGUS: Pardon Me?

ESTELLE: I have no time, Angus Fletcher, to discuss idiotic petitions.

ANGUS: I need to talk about street vendors.

ESTELLE: Your petition IS about street vendors.

ANGUS: Dad said you told him about my petition.

ESTELLE: Did your daddy do as I requested and talk sense into you?

ANGUS: He has no clue what sense is.

ESTELLE: That attracted your mama to him. Sit. Just cause you're seated, don't give you reason to expect to stay. Sixty seconds and you're out.

(ANGUS sits)

ESTELLE: *(Pause)* Well?

ANGUS: Dad said you have reports that the two vendors are wanted in Tennessee and Louisiana.

ESTELLE: Investigations are under way. I can't comment.

ANGUS: You told Dad.

ESTELLE: Your daddy takes small bits of information and embellishes 'em.

ANGUS: Every hour of the day.

ESTELLE: What concern are these vendors to you?

ANGUS: GJ wants to propose to one of them.

ESTELLE: You are pulling my chain. Lord have mercy that boy.

ANGUS: Dad believes they are after GJ's trust fund money.

ESTELLE: I warned you they was trash.

ANGUS: Dad wants to kill 'em.

ESTELLE: He has plans to kill everybody in this county. Began after Louise passed away.

ANGUS: Because he believes people framed Mom.

ESTELLE: Louise was my best friend. The two of us weren't angels growing up, so let me confirm ... your mama was not framed.

ANGUS: You don't know. Maybe Mom and Clifford were sitting in that Lincoln having a heart-to-heart talk. Mom dished out parental-type advice to all my friends.

ESTELLE: Parental advice?

ANGUS: Possibly. Probably. Definitely.

ESTELLE: They had no clothes on.

ANGUS: Maybe not.

ESTELLE: Your mama was the horniest woman in five counties. Good-hearted. She would do anything for any human being or animal. Charitable. But when it come to sex, Louise Daugherty Fletcher had not one ounce of judgment. Did you and GJ inherit your mama's hyper-sexual nature?

ANGUS: Nowhere close.

ESTELLE: I care about you, son. I care about GJ as much as it is possible to reach that boy.

ANGUS: I am going crazy, Miss Estelle. I am so confused.

ESTELLE: It's a mixed-up world, son.

ANGUS: This town is fucked up. No disrespect intended.

ESTELLE: I could open your eyes to how "fucked up" this town really is. But you sound fragile this moment.

ANGUS: I found someone I care about. Someone who lifts me to feel good about myself. Now I learn that person is a criminal. And Dad wants to kill him.

ESTELLE: HIM?

ANGUS: Or scare him off with one of your little fertilizer bombs.

ESTELLE: I don't know what you're talking about.

ANGUS: The way you scare crows.

ESTELLE: I still don't know what—

ANGUS: —Maybe you shoot crows, maybe you blow 'em up. I don't know, but I do know I don't trust that Daugherty is a respectable town. I don't trust there will be someone who will deeply love me. I don't trust my parents were sane. One was a sex-maniac pedophile, and one a conspiracy theorist who blames pickle-canning difficulties on Cubans. I don't trust I can judge people.

ESTELLE: "Him." You said, "scare him."

ANGUS: YES HIM! A guy. A man. A human being with a penis.

ESTELLE: Settle down, Angus. You caught me by surprise, that's all. What's your daddy say?

ANGUS: He got down on his knees and prayed I would never act upon "who I am."

ESTELLE: Life gits complicated … feels overwhelming … but me and you are going to figure out this thing together.

ANGUS: How? How are me and you gonna figure out this thing together?

ESTELLE: It'll come to us.

ANGUS: Right. It'll come to us. I gotta go. *(Walking toward door)* Oh yeah, Dad said to tell you he wants an extra-large order of roses.

ESTELLE: Hallelujah! There is a merciful God! It came to us!

ANGUS: What came to us?

ESTELLE: I am going to tell you something, Angus Winslow Daugherty Fletcher, that I have never, ever told nobody before.

(ANGUS nods)

ESTELLE: Will you allow me that?

(ANGUS nods)

ESTELLE: Can you keep my secret?

(ANGUS nods)

ESTELLE: Swear on Louise's grave.

ANGUS: *(Pause)* I swear on Mom's grave.

ESTELLE: Let me see your eyes when you're swearin' on yer mama's grave, son.

ANGUS: *(Staring into ESTELLE'S eyes)* I swear!

ESTELLE: Are you calm now?

ANGUS: I'm fine now, yes ma'am. No longer fragile.

ESTELLE: I do not have little fertilizer bombs.

ANGUS: I never believed you did.

ESTELLE: What I have is a bit bigger than that.

ANGUS: A bit?

ESTELLE: Hell of a lot bigger.

INTERMISSION

DAUGHTERTY PARK MERRY-GO-ROUND

ACT TWO
SCENE ONE

Setting: Gil's shooting range. Day. GIL is teaching GJ to shoot a pistol at targets. ESTELLE is nearby, hiding behind a bush.

GIL: Okay, hold it steady ... Slowly squeeze that trigger.

(GJ squeezes trigger)

GJ: Got it.

GIL: You shot the whiskey bottle?

GJ: The mailbox.

GIL: Supposed to shoot the bottle.

GJ: I like that purple mailbox. Where did you get that one?

GIL: Sort'a borrowed it from an old lady school teacher cross town. She never got mail nohow. Now focus on that there whiskey bottle.

(GJ aims pistol)

GIL: Steady ... steady ...

GJ: Slowly squeeze.

(He squeezes trigger)

GJ: *(Calmly)* Got it.

GIL: Good, son. Proud'a you.

GJ: When do I get to use bullets?

GIL: Shooting is about what happens up here. *(Pointing at his forehead)* All up here. If you hold strong focus on your target ... you don't need no bullets to prove it. You shot it good.

GJ: I shot it well. Dannon's teaching me to speak good.

GIL: Dannon?

GJ: I mean Shannon.

GIL: Let's talk about this Shannon lady. She your girlfriend?

GJ: I ain't never had no girlfriend fore.

GIL: Do you like this Shannon?

(GJ flaps his hands with excitement)

GJ: I claw-grabbed her a teddy whale.

GIL: Stop flappin'.

GJ: Theraphosidae, Phoneutria, Argiope Aurantia—

GIL: —Stop that! You know I don't like you namin' spiders.

GJ: Life is good, life is good, life is good—

GIL: —Stop that! Now hold it together. Does this woman like you?

GJ: She got me chocolate marshmallow.

GIL: Do you sleep together?

GJ: Fun naps.

GIL: What are "fun naps?"

GJ: She plays with Mr. Mickey.

GIL: Did you like how Mr. Mickey felt?

GJ: Better than when I thump him.

GIL: Lots'a men never learn that. Does Shannon ever put Mr. Mickey ... inside?

GJ: Inside what?

GIL: Women don't have Mr. Mickeys. They have a ... a place. Sometimes men put Mr. Mickeys in that ... into that place.

GJ: Why?

GIL: Stirs up more trouble than mortal man can imagine. I take it you and this Shannon don't do that.

GJ: She pats the top of my head.

GIL: Does she ask about your money?

GJ: She gives me quarters.

GIL: Does she ask about your trust funds?

GJ: Granddaddy Daugherty money?

GIL: Exactly.

GJ: I guess so.

GIL: Does she want to marry you?

GJ: I can't tell you, sir. *(Whispering)* It's our secret.

GIL: Okay. *(Whispering)* Don't tell me. *(Regular voice)* I have a carton of mint chocolate chip in the freezer. Help yourself.

GJ: Thank you, sir.

(He walks toward house)

GIL: Don't leave the carton out to melt!

GJ: I won't. Angus learn … taught me that.

(He exits)

GIL: Bout ice-cream. Not bout facts'a life.

(ESTELLE enters from behind bush)

GIL: You catch all that?

ESTELLE: Sadly, yes I did.

GIL: Then you know what we gotta do.

ESTELLE: We'll be breaking both yer sons' hearts.

GIL: What can I say? ... That's parenting.

End of Scene

DAUGHERTY PARK MERRY-GO-ROUND

ACT TWO
SCENE TWO

Setting: Angus's and GJ's kitchen. Day. ANGUS, sitting at table, picks at his food. GJ enters.

ANGUS: Where the heck have you been? When you wake before me, you're supposed to wait for me.

GJ: Dad was teaching me. See? I got it right: teaching.

ANGUS: Good.

GJ: Teaching me to shoot an old lady school teacher's mailbox.

ANGUS: Not good.

GJ: I hit the mailbox and whiskey bottle every time. Even with no bullets.

ANGUS: Been there. Done that.

(They point at their foreheads and laugh)

GJ and ANGUS: "All up here."

ANGUS: Did you see Shannon today?

GJ: She won't give me quarters if I tell.

ANGUS: Well, you gotta have quarters, so make sure you don't tell me about uh ... about uh ...

GJ: Marriage.

ANGUS: About marriage. You mean the secret about Robby Yates and Phyllis Lockhart's marriage, or the secret about you and Shannon's marriage?

GJ: Not Robby and Phyllis.

ANGUS: Good thing you didn't tell me.

GJ: You mad at me for not telling you, Angus?

ANGUS: I promise, Gerald Ralph Fletcher Junior, I am not mad at you.

GJ: I ate mint chocolate chip.

ANGUS: I see it round your mouth.

(GJ vigorously wipes mouth)

ANGUS: Where is Shannon?

GJ: Borrowin' a car from Lynn Jo's Used Cars and Tractors.

ANGUS: Let's hope it's: "to borrow." Why does she need a car?

GJ: Not South Carolina.

ANGUS: "Not South Carolina" ... Oh ... You wouldn't be fibbing to me, would you Gilbert Ralph Fletcher Junior? Nooooooo. Not you.

(GJ laughs and shrugs)

ANGUS: You know GJ, South Carolina is a fun-time state. Spanish moss up in the trees, spiders—lots of spiders. If you go to South Carolina, you can get a new cluster of spiders.

GJ: Tell Shannon to get me a cluster, Angus.

ANGUS: You tell her. If you go on a secret trip soon.

GJ: Is Wednesday soon?

ANGUS: Pretty soon. Five days.

GJ: Do I have a ID, Angus?

ANGUS: A state ID for trips and whatever?

GJ: Uh huh.

ANGUS: I keep it somewhere safe ... I bet you are thinking, "Now how do I get that ID from my brother Angus?"

(GJ makes no eye contact, nods with embarrassment)

ANGUS: GJ Fletcher? You are one sneaky fellow, yes you are.

GJ: I ain't sneaky. Not no way.

ANGUS: You go around saying, "not no way" and all these ignorant ways of talking. I teach you better. Why do you persist on talking like that?

GJ: I gotta fit in, Angus.

ANGUS: How does imprecise grammar help you fit in?

GJ: At the shelter.

ANGUS: Folks at Avery School talk like that?

GJ: Most of them folks. I mean those folks.

ANGUS: See. You know better.

GJ: I don't like them makin' fun'a me, Angus. Are you mad at me?

ANGUS: No, GJ, not mad. We all need to fit in.

GJ: Where do you fit?

ANGUS: Me? Someday … maybe I'll fit in at college.

GJ: Me and you can buy a house at your college.

ANGUS: That costs money.

GJ: When I turn 26, I get a million quarters.

ANGUS: A million quarters, huh? Lots of Juicy Fruit.

GJ: Not Juicy Fruit. A house.

ANGUS: I filled out my college application, but … I never mailed it in.

GJ: Cause you wanna stay here and fit in with James?

ANGUS: What?

GJ: "'You have been my best friend,' replied Charlotte. 'That in itself is a tremendous thing.'"

(ANGUS cries and cannot talk)

GJ: What's the matter, Angus? Did I say something bad?

(Angus shakes his head "no")

GJ: Don't cry. I'll tell you my secret.

ANGUS: I can't … I …

GJ: Can't what Angus? I can make it better.

ANGUS: You can't make it better, GJ. No one can.

GJ: I love you, Angus.

(He hugs ANGUS)

ANGUS: I know you do, big guy. It's such a mess, such a big mess.

GJ: I'll clean up the kitchen.

ANGUS: Not the kitchen, you big cucumber. Life! My life is a big mess.

GJ: I have two quarters in my pocket. I'll give you one.

ANGUS: If all you owned in the world were two quarters, you'd give them both to me, wouldn't you?

GJ: Just one.

ANGUS: I thought I was unhappy a few weeks ago when it was just you and me. I didn't know I had it so good. *(Crying)* Now my heart is … torn up.

GJ: Can somebody fix it?

ANGUS: Excellent question. I should try, huh? To fix it.

GJ: How did it get torn up?

ANGUS: Well, I uh … uh, I loved someone, a person, and uh …

GJ: James.

ANGUS: I never fool you.

(GJ strongly shakes head)

ANGUS: I love James. But I … James is messed-up … a bad person. He only pretends to be good.

GJ: Make believe?

ANGUS: Make believe.

GJ: Cuz he wants to be good.

ANGUS: What do you mean?

GJ: James makes believe he's good, so one day he can be good.

ANGUS: Wish it worked that way.

GJ: If you make believe enough, one day you do it.

ANGUS: Where did you learn that?

GJ: I make believe I can shoot. Then one day I will shoot good. I mean well. That's why we shoot with no bullets, ain't it?

(ANGUS has a blank stare. GJ repeatedly slaps the top of his head.)

GJ: I figured it out wrong! I hate that, I hate that!

ANGUS: No, no, GJ. Stop that ... You figured it out totally right, buddy. I missed it. I'll be danged ... beyond the jar ... *(Hurrying to leave)* I gotta go.

GJ: Where to?

ANGUS: Swimming.

(He runs out the door)

GJ: You don't got yer swim trunks!

ANGUS: *(Yelling back)* Don't need 'em!

GJ: *(To self)* He'll sunburn Mr. Mickey.

End of Scene

DAUGHERTY PARK MERRY-GO-ROUND

ACT TWO
SCENE THREE

Setting: Daugherty Park near pond. Night. JAMES and ANGUS, sitting on blanket, are looking straight ahead.

ANGUS: And Estelle showed the police report to my dad. How Shannon married two older men, how they died, how you guys got the money, are on the lam.

JAMES: Her older sister swindled those old men.

ANGUS: Save it! Every lie's one more dagger.

JAMES: I'm not sticking it to you.

ANGUS: Yes or no? Shannon is your sister.

JAMES: *(Pause)* Not.

ANGUS: Is her name really Shannon?

JAMES: Beatrice. She hates that name.

ANGUS: Is your name really James?

JAMES: In school I was "Jimmy." But yeah.

ANGUS: Are you two trying to get GJ's and my trust funds?

JAMES: Yeah.

ANGUS: So, all of this friendship, you and me … is what?

JAMES: Beatrice tried, but couldn't get you excited—putting it politely.

ANGUS: So, you stepped up to the plate?

JAMES: Believe me, Angus, I'm not after your funds. Not no more.

ANGUS: So, I should forget this past month happened.

JAMES: I want to stay your friend.

(ANGUS turns away. JAMES stares intensely at him. After a moment ANGUS looks at JAMES.)

JAMES: ... For the rest of my life.

ANGUS: How can you look me straight in my eyes and lie like that?

JAMES: I'm not lying. I never said anything like that to nobody before. Especially not no guy.

ANGUS: God I wanna believe you.

JAMES: Believe me, Angus.

(ANGUS stands, walks a few feet away)

JAMES: I'll do anything.

ANGUS: Anything?

(JAMES nods)

ANGUS: Anything?

JAMES: Anything.

ANGUS: Okay. *(Pause)* Here it is.

JAMES: Okay.

ANGUS: Tonight ... here in Daugherty Park ... on this blanket ... you and me ... have sex.

JAMES: *(Quick to agree)* Okay ... *(Second thoughts)* Angus? ... Name something else. Not that.

ANGUS: If you don't, I'll go to the police.

JAMES: *(Quietly resigned)* Go ... I can't.

ANGUS: Golly!!! ... That's the one answer that makes me believe you wanna be my friend.

(He cries. JAMES walks on his knees to ANGUS and hugs him around the knees.)

JAMES: I am your friend, Angus, honest to God. I'll do anything to keep you, well except, anything else … I love you.

ANGUS: I love you too, man … What are we gonna do?

(He gets down on his knees and they hug)

JAMES: Be idiots together?

ANGUS: I love being an idiot with you.

End of Scene

ACT TWO

SCENE FOUR

Setting: Estelle's Flower Company. Night. There are roses and shovels. GIL struggles to sit, cautiously protecting his back.

GIL: Ahhh.

ESTELLE: Gracious Gil. You should had let my Mexicans shovel all that cow crap into the trailer. Now you gone and hurt yourself.

GIL: Be good as new in a month or two.

ESTELLE: My Mexicans are young and strong.

GIL: They're from Mexico.

ESTELLE: That's why they're Mexicans.

GIL: Mexico is near Cuba.

ESTELLE: So is Florida.

GIL: I don't trust Floridians.

ESTELLE: You don't trust nobody, Gil.

GIL: I trust you. Always will. You sure your bomb's gonna work?

ESTELLE: Of course, it will. We'll discreetly drive up beside those two criminals—

GIL: —"Discreetly?" An 18-wheeler painted with "Estelle's Roses" on the side?

ESTELLE: I own forty-three semis, Gil. I reported that particular truck stolen. Filed off its serial number. We'll block their path, get out, use my smart-phone detonator, blow the entire kit and caboodle.

GIL: It's a mighty big bomb, Estelle.

ESTELLE: Will blow an asteroid-size crater. They'll never identify there was a car beside my vaporized truck, much less there was humans inside.

GIL: My family fell upon hard times, Estelle. God bless you. You're here for me and my boys.

ESTELLE: Louise would want me to do this for her boys. God rest her soul.

GIL: Amen to that. Louise loved those boys.

ESTELLE: That she did.

GIL: Loved their friends too.

ESTELLE: That she … did too.

(GIL looks to the heavens as if in prayer)

GIL: Louise, darling, all this work we did, me and Estelle, although it's gonna help GJ and Angus, this is for you, baby doll. Hope you're looking down and is proud of us. Amen.

ESTELLE: Amen.

(GIL groans and rubs his back, clearly in pain)

GIL: You got Advil?

ESTELLE: Tylenol.

GIL: Gotta have my Advil.

ESTELLE: Got Oxycontin.

GIL: *(Shaking head no)* Clogs my sewer pipe. *(Pause)* Where'd I go wrong, Estelle? I played all my fathering cards.

ESTELLE: Sometimes, God hands us what we don't understand. GJ was just born that way.

GIL: I'm meanin' Angus.

ESTELLE: What's wrong with Angus?

GIL: He didn't tell you?

ESTELLE: Him lovin' that street vendor boy?

GIL: Him avoiding college.

ESTELLE: No! Oh, that's terrible! Tragic!

GIL: College got me to where I am today.

ESTELLE: Huh ... Maybe after we blow up this fella, Angus'll decide on college.

GIL: He's too dad-gone consumed looking after GJ.

ESTELLE: I hear it in his voice. Angus loves GJ to death ... Now this carnie.

GIL: Well, at least that's a first step. Practicing on this fella.

ESTELLE: Then maybe move on to a woman.

GIL: Woman, man, dog, goat, anything. Let go'a GJ and move on.

ESTELLE: But it wuz good he looked after GJ.

GIL: Plum good. But too long is too long. He's dying inside and can't see it. I struggle with gittin' him to grasp that big picture.

ESTELLE: Your pickle jar talk?

GIL: And other talks.

ESTELLE: I'm comforted to know you have other talks.

GIL: Simple as GJ is, at least he's capable'a lovin' outside hisself.

ESTELLE: The sister?

GIL: Spiders.

ESTELLE: Oh yeah. Spiders.

GIL: Named 'em. Scientific and personal names: Sophie, Rhonda Sue, Betsy, Moby.

ESTELLE: And now GJ loves a street vendor girl. That's outside hisself too. Both yer sons finally got somebody human to love.

GIL: Until we vaporize 'em.

ESTELLE: Won't be hide nor hair left ...You sure we oughta do this?

GIL: Hmm ... I know we reasoned our reasons earlier. But right this minute, my mind can't wrap itself around how we concluded what we concluded. But we did conclude it, so we musta concluded it for some good reason. Let it be. Besides, it'll be a hell of a crater.

ESTELLE: It will, Gilbert Fletcher, oh my golly it will.

End of Scene

ACT TWO

SCENE FIVE

Setting: Food cart on Brine Street. Day. JAMES and SHANNON are walking and talking.

JAMES: They know everything. That one old guy choked on a strawberry. One drowned in ice-cream-maker water.

SHANNON: Wow was that luck.

JAMES: Luck had a helping hand.

SHANNON: I'm hurt you think I'd harm two sweet old men.

JAMES: Right. Just like you wouldn't steal nobody's trust funds.

SHANNON: They don't know my plan to drive GJ to South Carolina, do they?

JAMES: Angus called it: "transporting his incapacitated brother across state lines."

SHANNON: You told Angus, you asshole!

JAMES: These people are smart. To them we're transparent.

SHANNON: Fine. I'll salvage this job solo.

JAMES: By marrying an intellectually deficient man boy?

SHANNON: "Intellectually deficient?" You changed your entire speech patterns. The way you dress. You switched sides on me, Jimmy. Is sex really that good with Angus?

(JAMES slaps SHANNON)

SHANNON: Fuck! It's not sex. It's love.

JAMES: You're clueless.

SHANNON: Clueless? I know you and Angus gotta be grinding away. You don't never touch me no more.

JAMES: I don't "touch" you, cause you became this maniac bitch.

SHANNON: While you became Angus's soft-hearted bitch.

JAMES: I'll hit you again. I swear.

SHANNON: Hit me, Jimmy. Prove you're "the man" cause you beat up women. I'm turning my other cheek to you, homo. Right here.

(JAMES punches his fist into his other palm)

SHANNON: If I teamed up with Marty or Ruben, I'd never suggest they hook up with Angus. They'd chop me into little pieces. But you and Angus? Woman's intuition.

(JAMES slowly walks away)

SHANNON: Going back to your boyfriend? Cry on his shoulder?

JAMES: I'm leaving.

SHANNON: That sounds like you mean, "leaving for good."

JAMES: Your woman's intuition is getting it right.

SHANNON: If you walk away, Jimmy, that's it. And if you take "that's it" to mean "that's it for good," your woman's intuition's getting it right.

JAMES: Stay away from GJ.

SHANNON: Tell me Jimmy: after you "orgasm" and you flashback to your nights at the orphanage, get all freaky, does that fascinate Angus? Bewitch him to rescue carnie trash?

JAMES: You are one cruel person.

SHANNON: One what?

JAMES: One … cruel … person.

SHANNON: No cussing? No beating? Just: "You are one cruel person." You grew weak, Jimmy. I despise weak.

JAMES: Angus is teaching me to be strong. You have no idea what really being strong is.

(He exits. SHANNON packs the food cart. GJ enters.)

GJ: Hi Shannon.

SHANNON: How's the only man I like on this lopsided planet?

GJ: Me?

SHANNON: You GJ. Nobody else.

GJ: You love James.

SHANNON: Not no more.

GJ: I love you. And James, and Angus, and Sophie.

SHANNON: You treat women with kindness, make a woman feel on a pedestal. It's not about sex. Not about money or power. Simple. Pure. Kinda like dating an angel.

GJ: Angels date?

SHANNON: Say? Remember those spiders you told me about?

GJ: Arachnids.

SHANNON: Those ones.

GJ: I can name all of 'em.

SHANNON: Before? I was scared to look at crawly spiders, but now? I'm more curiouser.

GJ: I'm glad you're more curiouser. I'll show you Vern. He's a banana spider. They travel on bananas in boats. Real name is "Brazil Wandering Spider." Phoneutria. You can't hold Vern in yer hand. He's got strong venom.

SHANNON: Got any tarantulas? Like in *Indiana Jones*?

GJ: Sophie. Giant tarantula. Theraphosidae. She's my favorite. Hairy.

SHANNON: Ooooh. Sounds better than a gun.

GJ: I gotta gun.

SHANNON: You gotta gun, GJ?

GJ: At Dad's.

SHANNON: Do you know how to shoot it?

GJ: Every Saturday. Never miss.

SHANNON: You are the man, GJ.

(She puts her arm around GJ's waist as they walk)

SHANNON: Definitely the man. Damn. Life on this planet's looking up. Tilting my direction.

(They exit)

End of Scene

DAUGHERTY PARK MERRY-GO-ROUND

ACT TWO
SCENE SIX

Setting: Angus's and GJ's kitchen. Night. GJ is eating ice cream when ANGUS enters.

ANGUS: Where in tarnation have you been for two days? I looked everywhere.

GJ: Did you look in South Carolina?

ANGUS: Oh my God. Beatrice—I mean Shannon—kidnapped you.

GJ: She engaged me.

ANGUS: What does "engaged you" mean?

GJ: I give Shannon my blue ring from the claw-grab machine. Just took one quarter. Not counting quarters fore Wednesday.

ANGUS: She kidnapped you.

GJ: No naps.

ANGUS: Not nap. Kidnapped. Took you by force, took you hostage, abducted you.

GJ: She drove me.

ANGUS: Where?

GJ: In her rented Mini Cooper.

ANGUS: To South Carolina?

GJ: Uh huh.

ANGUS: Did she marry you?

GJ: Nope.

ANGUS: No?

GJ: She said, "I do."

ANGUS: Oh my gosh. What did you say?

GJ: I told her, Aunt Phoebe said, "Anyone who has less than twelve bridesmaids dressed in lemon chiffon shouldn't be permitted to marry."

ANGUS: Aunt Phoebe said that?

GJ: At cousin Louis's wedding.

ANGUS: But did YOU say, "I do?"

GJ: There weren't no music, no cake, no church, not even no ice cream. No guests—Not even you, Angus. How could I?

(ANGUS pauses, breaks into laughter)

GJ: What's funny?

ANGUS: What did Shannon do?

GJ: Run outta the courthouse screamin'.

ANGUS: Oh my gosh, I wish I coulda been there.

GJ: Did I do bad, Angus?

ANGUS: You did fantastic, big brother.

GJ: She got madder than Miss Estelle that time you insulted her.

ANGUS: Estelle. I forgot about Estelle. Where are Shannon and James?

GJ: Shannon brung me home, went to find James. Said she wuz gonna kill 'im.

ANGUS: In a pretend voice or a serious voice?

GJ: Oh, she wuz mad, Angus. Her real voice.

ANGUS: Where did she go?

GJ: I don't know. I got me this ice cream outta yer freezer. Hope you ain't mad.

ANGUS: Eat all the ice cream you want, bug guy.

(He walks toward the door)

GJ: Tell her to bring back my spider she stole!!!

(ANGUS stops)

ANGUS: She took one of your spiders?

GJ: In a mason jar. I showed her Vern—

ANGUS: —The banana spider??? Shit. James is deathly allergic to spiders!

(He hurriedly exits. GJ scoops ice cream as he talks to self.)

GJ: But she stole my favorite. I swear she better not hurt Sophie.

End of Scene

DAUGHERTY PARK MERRY-GO-ROUND

ACT TWO
SCENE SEVEN

Setting: Daugherty Park near pond. Later that night. JAMES'S body is lying on the ground. SHANNON, sitting at a distance, is holding an empty mason jar. ANGUS hurriedly enters, runs to JAMES'S side and kneels.

ANGUS: Oh my God no. James? God no.

SHANNON: You're too late.

ANGUS: *(Startles)* What did you do?

SHANNON: I took this little jar, unscrewed this little lid, tossed GJ's spider on Jimmy's neck, and laughed my ass off.

ANGUS: He's allergic to spiders!

SHANNON: I'm the one who told you that.

ANGUS: James, no, no.

SHANNON: He'll be whining and obnoxious in a minute.

ANGUS: What do you mean?

SHANNON: I threw Sophie on him and—

ANGUS: —Sophie?

SHANNON: Big hairy tarantula?

ANGUS: Sophie won't bite anything no matter what you do.

SHANNON: I know that NOW. Should'a gone with Vern the banana spider.

ANGUS: He's not dead?

(He checks JAMES'S carotid artery for pulse)

SHANNON: He fainted. Big tough gangster, ain't he? A baby lamb in wolf's clothing.

(ANGUS begins gently slapping JAMES'S face)

ANGUS: James, James, wake up buddy.

SHANNON: Can't hurry him out of his fainting spells.

ANGUS: He's fainted before?

SHANNON: Duh. After every orgasm.

ANGUS: What???

SHANNON: Course you know that.

ANGUS: Why would I know that?

SHANNON: He loves you!

ANGUS: We're friends. Real friends. Not make believe like you pretending to be brother and sister.

SHANNON: We are brother and sister.

ANGUS: I read the police report, "Beatrice."

SHANNON: Or maybe not.

ANGUS: How long does he stay passed out?

SHANNON: Three and a half minutes. Could be longer this time. Sophie's one scary bug.

ANGUS: Poor guy.

(He walks to SHANNON and sits by her)

ANGUS: Where is Sophie?

SHANNON: Crawled off that way.

(She hands jar to ANGUS)

ANGUS: GJ loves Sophie.

SHANNON: GJ loves a bug. Figures.

ANGUS: Heard the wedding didn't go as planned.

SHANNON: I'm the fuckin' biggest idiot to ever say "I do" in front of a Justice of the Peace. GJ gave me this.

(She shows off her large blue plastic ring)

ANGUS: He was excited to claw-grab that ring for you.

(He sniffs the air and makes a sour face)

ANGUS: I apologize for saying this, but … you smell like crap.

(He moves away a small distance)

SHANNON: There was a ... incident.

ANGUS: Involving crap?

SHANNON: GJ was crying hard, cause when he jilted me, I screamed a string of … you know. I stopped at his favorite spot to buy him ice cream so he would quit crying and apologizing so fucking non-stop.

ANGUS: Been there many times.

SHANNON: GJ went into the ice-cream store; I stayed in the Mini Cooper. Suddenly a big tractor-trailer from that Rose Company …

ANGUS: Estelle's Roses.

SHANNON: Pulled in front of me, backed up to my car. A lady in a black gown with a Lone Ranger mask jumped out, opened the back of the truck. I was staring at this gigantic pile of cow shit with giant candle things jammed into it. The broad ran across the parking lot to some guy in a Lone Ranger mask who yelled, "Pay Back Time Fidel!" I thought: "What the fuck?" Wouldn't you think: "What the fuck?"

ANGUS: I would.

SHANNON: The broad held out a phone, then came this big whoosh sound. WOOSH … Three tons of cow shit almost buried me in my Mini Cooper.

ANGUS: No!

SHANNON: Fucking cow shit.

ANGUS: Fertilizer. Those two Lone Rangers were trying to kill you.

SHANNON: With cow shit?

ANGUS: They ain't the world's foremost bomb makers.

SHANNON: "Whoosh." GJ and I hiked back to your house. I asked him to put a spider in a mason jar for me.

ANGUS: Sophie.

SHANNON: I ran out with Sophie and hunted down Jimmy.

ANGUS: You really wanted to kill him?

SHANNON: He's a fuckin' slime ball. *(Yells to James)* You're a fuckin' slime ball, Jimmy!

JAMES: Oooh.

(ANGUS rushes to JAMES'S side)

ANGUS: James. You okay, buddy?

(He helps JAMES to sit)

JAMES: How did I get on the ground?

SHANNON: *(Yells)* I screwed up fuckin' killing you, that's how.

JAMES: Kill me?

SHANNON: *(Yells)* You fucked up my whole life with your fuckin' get-rich schemes.

JAMES: *(Yells)* Get a job like normal people do.

SHANNON: *(Yells)* This is my job, normal-person asshole.

JAMES: I musta tripped. Hit my head. Am I bleeding?

ANGUS: Don't see any blood.

JAMES: Is my face messed up?

ANGUS: Handsome as always.

JAMES: Thank God.

SHANNON: You fainted Jimmy!

JAMES: I didn't faint.

SHANNON: You fuckin' fainted cuz I threw a fuckin' big hairy tarantula on you. A big hairy …

(JAMES faints)

SHANNON: He's out.

(ANGUS slaps JAMES'S face)

ANGUS: James, James.

SHANNON: Waste'a energy.

ANGUS: He didn't even see Sophie again.

SHANNON: He's got high-octane imagination.

ANGUS: Like my dad.

SHANNON: Let me ask you. I thought gay guys was supposed to be best friends with women friends, not with tough gangster guys.

ANGUS: That lump of body on the ground, who keeps fainting, is a tough gangster guy?

SHANNON: In Jimmy's head, he thinks if he pretends to be tough, one day he'll be tough.

ANGUS: Huh. That philosophy's starting to grow on me … So, if he faints every time he … you know.

SHANNON: Blows his wad?

ANGUS: That. Why does he bother?

SHANNON: If it can walk, he'll screw it. If he was standing on the edge of a high cliff with a goat, even if he knew he would fall to his death, he'd screw the goat. If you tied him down to a four-poster bed, he'd find a way. Course I'm no shrink, but I think after Jimmy passes out, he don't remember he had sex.

ANGUS: So … every time is like his first time?

SHANNON: Perpetual horny virgin.

ANGUS: Makes two of us.

SHANNON: You two really don't do the big nasty.

ANGUS: Nope.

SHANNON: Amazing ... Jimmy must respect you something big.

ANGUS: You think so?

SHANNON: *(Yells)* I hate your fuckin' guts, Jimmy Bartolomucci!

ANGUS: That's his last name?

SHANNON: This month.

JAMES: Oooh.

(ANGUS rushes to JAMES)

ANGUS: James, James.

JAMES: How did I get on the ground?

SHANNON: I fuckin' tossed a—

ANGUS: —You fell! That's all buddy. You fell.

JAMES: I musta tripped. Hit my head. Am I bleeding?

ANGUS: Let me see.

(He examines JAMES'S head)

ANGUS: Don't see any blood.

JAMES: Is my face messed up?

ANGUS: Handsome as always.

JAMES: Thank God. Let me up.

ANGUS: Maybe you should sit a while.

JAMES: Nothin' to it.

(ANGUS helps JAMES to his feet)

SHANNON: Jimmy? I hate your fuckin' guts.

JAMES: Baby, I tripped and hit my head. I'm suffering over here. Go nice on me.

SHANNON: How's this for, "Go nice on you?"

(SHANNON pulls out the pistol and points it at JAMES)

JAMES: Whoa! That thing could go off, baby.

SHANNON: It's gonna go off. It's gonna splatter your brains all over the fuckin' merry-go-round.

ANGUS: Let's the three of us talk this out.

SHANNON: Shut the fuck up, AGNES.

JAMES: She's unhappy. Not her monthly irritable drama, you know. Big-time pissed.

SHANNON: Sexist! Shut up! Both'a ya!

JAMES: We're quiet, we're quiet, right Angus? We're quiet.

ANGUS: Guns are dangerous.

SHANNON: You think?

JAMES: Yeah baby, you may hurt yourself. Break a fingernail or something.

SHANNON: I ain't gonna be the one hurting.

ANGUS: What do you want from us?

SHANNON: I want him to die.

ANGUS: Killing him won't make you feel better.

SHANNON: Shut up! ... On second thought, Agnes is right.

ANGUS: Angus.

SHANNON: Killing you won't make me feel better.

(She points the pistol at JAMES'S crotch)

JAMES: Whoa, whoa. What the heck?

SHANNON: I'm gonna blow off your dick.

JAMES: You like my dick.

SHANNON: Really? I said those words, “I like your dick?”

JAMES: You drew it on a valentine and colored it for me.

SHANNON: Oh yeah. I did. It was awesome. And now it won’t be.

(She waves the pistol back and forth)

SHANNON: Was. Won’t be. Was. Won’t be.

JAMES: Please, Beatrice, please.

SHANNON: Never call me that!!!

JAMES: Okay, okay, okay I won’t. Shannon.

SHANNON: This’ll feel real good for me, Jimmy. Not for your boys, but for me? Real good.

JAMES: Where the heck did you get a gun?

SHANNON: GJ.

JAMES: GJ???

ANGUS: That’s GJ’s pistol?

SHANNON: His target practice pistol.

ANGUS: You’re positive that’s GJ’s pistol?

SHANNON: The handle’s gooey with chocolate marshmallow.

(She squints as she concentrates and aims the pistol at JAMES’S groin)

SHANNON: “Just squeeze the trigger real steady.” Like Grandma Buffalo Annie taught me in the circus. “Steady … aim …”

JAMES: No, baby doll. Anything you want.

SHANNON: And slowly … squeeze ...

(The moment SHANNON pulls the trigger, she lunges forward with the gun and screams)

SHANNON: BAM!!!

(JAMES yells as he grabs his crotch and bends at the waist)

JAMES: Ah!

(After a moment, he falls to his knees in pain, holding his crotch)

JAMES: Oh God, Angus. My dick and balls are gone.

(He rolls over, lands on his back, remains motionless)

SHANNON: *(Pause, calmly)* I didn't hear no bang. Did you hear a bang?

(She examines the pistol)

SHANNON: What happened to the bang?

ANGUS: GJ's pistol doesn't make a bang.

SHANNON: What gun doesn't make a bang?

ANGUS: Special silencer. Dad's protective of his ears.

SHANNON: Very fatherly. My grandma never gave a flyin' ...

(She pauses and studies JAMES from a distance)

SHANNON: He ain't hurt bad, is he?

ANGUS: Men bleed profusely when their testicles and penises are ... traumatically removed.

SHANNON: I did not know that.

ANGUS: One hundred percent of the time, they die.

SHANNON: Die??? Oh shit!

ANGUS: You better leave before the police—

SHANNON: —Oh my God. I didn't mean to kill Jimmy. I only meant to ruin the rest of his life. Honest, Angus.

ANGUS: He had it coming.

SHANNON: You know he did. Son of a bitch. Jimmy, you fucking idiot, you made me do this!

ANGUS: He made you do it. Absolutely. You need to blow town now!

(SHANNON runs off stage yelling)

SHANNON: Oh my God!

(Suddenly, she calmly walks back onto stage and gently lays the pistol on the ground. She speaks very calmly and politely.)

SHANNON: Here's GJ's gun. Tell him I only borrowed it. Didn't steal it or nothing. But I'm keeping my ring. Hope he finds Sophie.

(She abruptly turns and runs off the stage yelling)

SHANNON: Oh my God!

ANGUS: *(Yells)* Run far as you can!

(He kneels and gently slaps JAMES'S face)

ANGUS: James, James.

JAMES: Oooh.

ANGUS: Sit up, pal.

(He helps JAMES to sit)

JAMES: How did I get on the ground?

(ANGUS hugs JAMES, who is comfortable with hug)

ANGUS: You fell. That's all, buddy. You fell.

JAMES: I musta tripped. Hit my head. Am I bleeding?

ANGUS: Don't see any blood.

JAMES: Is my face messed up?

ANGUS: Handsome as always.

JAMES: Thank God … *(Startles)* What was that?

ANGUS: What was what?

JAMES: Something moved.

ANGUS: Where?

JAMES: There in the leaves. Right there! See???

(He points at a specific spot on the ground)

ANGUS: Sophie! Thank God. GJ's spider.

(He places the mason jar upside down over Sophie and screws on the lid)

JAMES: Sophie?

ANGUS: His favorite Tarantula.

JAMES: Tarantula?

(He passes out. ANGUS gently slaps his face. GIL and ESTELLE enter wearing Lone Ranger masks. ESTELLE has her gardening bag.)

GIL: What the hell's going on? GJ's back at the house crying his heart out. Said Shannon stole his pistol, stole Sophie.

ANGUS: Shannon threw Sophie on James, then shot him in his privates with GJ's pistol.

ESTELLE: Oh my golly. What some people are capable of.

GIL: How the heck was he shot with GJ's pistol?

ANGUS: Rich imagination.

ESTELLE: He's not dead?

ANGUS: He thought he was ball-less, penis-less. So he fainted.

GIL: Well, when he gets unfainted, I'll render him dead. Estelle? Give me your rose-clippin' scissors.

(ESTELLE looks in her gardening bag. ANGUS stands and yells.)

ANGUS: Dad! Estelle! I want you to leave. Now!

GIL: We ain't completed our mission.

ANGUS: Murdering people with cow shit and rose scissors?

ESTELLE: Honey, me and your daddy are only trying to protect you and GJ. That's all, baby doll.

ANGUS: Both of you leave! NOW!

(He kneels and cuddles JAMES in his arms)

ANGUS: James is going to wake any minute, and for this moment, he's quiet, not ruining life with his loud, filthy mouth. So, in front of you, in sight of Mom's grave, in front of GOD, this silent moment is for me! ... I fit in!

GIL: Son, it's only a moment.

ANGUS: That's what I am, Dad. Moments.

ESTELLE: Gil, honey, let's go. Let Angus be his moment.

GIL: *(Nodding)* Okay son.

(He walks, stops, turns to ANGUS)

GIL: Did I tell you about the time I was a moment, back when the Grateful Dead—

ESTELLE: —Gil!

ANGUS: Dad!

(GIL nods, "Let's go." He and ESTELLE exit, his arm around ESTELLE'S shoulders. ANGUS cuddles JAMES as he looks to the sky.)

ANGUS: Thank you, God. I earned this moment. I deserve it, and you know it. So, let me have this moment. If you do, I vow to make it stick in my head, in my heart for as long as you let me live.

JAMES: Ooooh.

ANGUS: And my moment's gone.

(JAMES sits up)

JAMES: How did I get on the ground?

(ANGUS lifts Sophie's jar in front of JAMES'S face)

ANGUS: James, look at this. It's Sophie.

JAMES: That's a ... that' a—

ANGUS: —A big hairy tarantula.

(JAMES faints in ANGUS'S arms)

ANGUS: Sorry. I needed my moment to last longer ... Moments are short. Guess that's why they're moments ... You won't remember this ... but I will. You'll have other moments. I have this moment.

(He looks at sky)

ANGUS: There's our star ... Well, my star. Up there shining down on me ... on us ... Thank you, Mom.

(He continues to cuddle JAMES while looking at the sky)

FINALE

DC Fidler (Author)

A native of the North Carolina Appalachian Mountains, DC Fidler has combined a career in academic psychiatry and cultural psychiatry with a lifetime of playwriting, acting, directing, composing music, and teaching creative writing and the dramatic arts.

He studied theatre, writing, medicine, and psychiatry at the University of North Carolina at Chapel Hill, where he served on the faculty. He later served on the faculty at West Virginia University and also practiced psychiatry in Australia and New Zealand.

He began his acting career in outdoor dramas, summer stock theatre, and local films and television at age ten. He has written scripts and composed music for over fifty medical educational videos and his plays have been produced in community theatres, at universities, and in professional theatres in North Carolina, Virginia, Ohio, West Virginia, Alaska, St. Louis, Sacramento, San Diego, Los Angeles, Boston, Chicago, and New York City.

He consulted and appeared in educational productions for HBO, ABC, and PBS and performed in stage plays including: *Hope is the Thing with Feathers, Night of January 16th, Thieves' Carnival, Blood Wedding, Our Town, A Life in the Theatre*, and *Fool for Love.* DC Fidler is an active member of the Dramatists Guild of America and the Charlotte Writers' Club.

Fidler previously chaired the Video Committee for the American Psychiatric Association and served as President of the Association for Academic Psychiatry, promoting the use of arts in psychiatry. He was inducted as a Fellow of the Royal College of Physicians of Ireland and serves on the Arts and Humanities Committee for the Group for the Advancement of Psychiatry, co-producing a video series on the History of Psychiatry.

DC Fidler lived and worked with the Alutiiq tribe in Akhiok, Alaska, the Al Moqbali Bedouin tribe near Sohar, Oman, the Kalkadoon Tribe in the outback of Queensland, Australia, and the Te Tau Ihu Maori Tribes on the South Island of New Zealand.

He is author of the textbook, *Psychiatry for Actors: Building a Character Using Psychiatric Principles*, and author of the novels, *Boogieban* and *Wood Whisperers.*

Plays, Novels, and Textbooks by DC Fidler

Plays

- Voices in the Woods
- Guilt by Association (With RJ Casey)
- Three Diaries
- Sir William Bowlinggreen and Company
- Shiraz
- Anniversary of Miss Nanette Pringle
- School Children Hiding Under Desks
- Grams
- Camp Uni
- Boogieban (Two-Actor Version)
- Boogieban (Seven-Actor Version)
- Ahulaqs
- Elk and Wolf (With Travis Teffner)
- Santee Delta (With Travis Teffner)
- Celtic Crossing
- Stone Touchin'
- Daugherty Park Merry-Go-Round
- La Dynastie
- The Last Farm
- Gyges
- Begat

Short Plays

- Persons
- Cruise
- Mobile to Where
- Oman Truce
- Second Amendment
- The Greek God Club
- Five X
- Microscopic Misconceptions

- Drone Guns
- Moon Bugs (With Travis Teffner)

Screenplays

- Green Lights of Baghdad (with RJ Casey)

Musicals

- Pied Piper (With Lauren Horacek)
- Healer Man
- Medicine Show

Novels and Textbooks

- Boogieban
- Wood Whisperers
- Psychiatry for Actors: Building a Character Using Psychiatric Principles

www.ingramcontent.com/pod-product-compliance
Ingram Content Group UK Ltd.
Pitfield, Milton Keynes, MK11 3LW, UK
UKHW021656190726
13853UKWH00001B/290

9 798985 520958